20

JUNIOR

CLASSICS

Published in Red Turtle by
Rupa Publications India Pvt. Ltd 2016
7/16, Ansari Road, Daryaganj
New Delhi 110002

Sales centres:
Allahabad Bengaluru Chennai
Hyderabad Jaipur Kathmandu
Kolkata Mumbai

ISBN: 978-81-291-3954-2

Second impression 2017

10 9 8 7 6 5 4 3 2

Printed at Rakmo Press Pvt. Ltd, New Delhi

Contents

THE ADVENTURE

OF THE ABBEY GRANGE

Arthur Conan Doyle

On a frosty and cold winter morning of 1897, Holmes, tugging at my shoulder, awakened me.

'Come, Watson, come!' he cried. 'The game is afoot. Not a word! Into your clothes and come!'

Ten minutes later, we were both in a cab, on our way to Charing Cross Station. The air was bitterly cold, and it wasn't until we had taken our places in the Kentish train, that Holmes took out a note from his pocket, and read aloud:

Abbey Grange,
Marsham,
Kent,
3:30am

My Dear Mr. Holmes,

I should be very glad of your immediate assistance in what promises to be a most remarkable case. It is something quite in your line. Except for releasing the lady I will see that everything is kept exactly as I have found it, but I beg you not to lose an instant, as it is difficult to leave Sir Eustace there.

Yours faithfully,
Stanley Hopkins

'Our present research appears to be a case of murder,' said Holmes.

'You think this Sir Eustace is dead, then?'

'I should say so. Hopkins's writing shows considerable agitation, and he is not an emotional man. Yes, I gather there has been violence, and that the body is left for our inspection. A mere suicide would not have caused him to send for me. As to the release of the lady, it would appear that she has been locked in her room during the tragedy. I think that we shall have an interesting morning. Well, here we are at Chiselhurst Station, and we shall soon set our doubts at rest.'

A drive of a couple of miles brought us to a park gate, which was opened for us by an old lodge-keeper. The avenue ran through a park, and ended in a low, widespread house, pillared in front—typical Palladio architecture. The central part was evidently old and shrouded in ivy, but

one wing of the house appeared to be entirely new. The youthful and alert Inspector Stanley Hopkins confronted us in the open doorway.

'I'm very glad you have come, Mr Holmes. And you too, Dr Watson. But, I should not have troubled you, for since the lady has come to herself, she has given so clear an account of the affair that there is not much left for us to do. You remember that Lewisham gang of burglars?'

'What, the three Randalls?'

'Exactly— the father and two sons. It's their work. They did a job at Sydenham a fortnight ago and were seen and described. Rather cool to do another so soon and so near, but it is they, beyond all doubt.'

'Sir Eustace Brackenstall is dead, then?'

'Yes, his head was knocked in with his own poker.'

'He was one of the richest men in Kent— Lady Brackenstall has had the most dreadful experience. She seemed half dead when I saw her first. I think you had best see her and hear her account of the facts. Then we will examine the dining room together.'

Seldom have I seen so graceful a figure, so womanly a presence, and so beautiful a face as

Lady Brackenstall. She had golden hair and blue eyes, and would have had the perfect complexion, had not her recent experience left her drawn and haggard. She suffered a plum-coloured swelling over on eye, which her maid, Theresa—a tall, austere woman—was bathing assiduously with vinegar and water. The lady lay back exhausted upon a couch, but gave us a quick, observant gaze, as we entered the room. She wore a loose blue and silver dressing gown.

'I have told you all that happened, Mr Hopkins,' she said, wearily. 'Could you not repeat it? Well, if you think it necessary, I will tell these gentlemen what occurred. Have they been in the dining room yet?'

'I thought they had better hear your ladyship's story first.'

'I shall be glad when you can arrange matters. It is horrible for me to think of him still lying there.'

She shuddered and buried her face in her hands. As she did so, the loose gown fell back from her forearms. Holmes uttered an exclamation.

'You have other injuries, madam! What is this?'

Two vivid red spots stood out on one of the white, round limbs. She hastily covered it.

'It is nothing. It has no connection with this hideous business tonight. If you and your friend will sit down, I will tell you all I can.'

'I am the wife of Sir Eustace Brackenstall. I have been married about a year, and there's no point trying to conceal that ours wasn't a happy marriage. Perhaps the fault may be partly mine. I was brought up in the less-conventional atmosphere of South Australia, and this English life, with its proprieties and its primness, doesn't come naturally to me. But the main reason is that Sir Eustace was a confirmed drunkard. To be with such a man for an hour is unpleasant. Can you imagine what it means to be tied to him for day and night? It is a sacrilege, a crime to hold that such a marriage is binding,' she said, face red in anger, before being soothed by her maid.

'I will tell you about last night,' she continued.

'In this house all the servants sleep in the modern wing. This central block is made up of the dwelling-rooms, with the kitchen behind and our bedroom above. My maid sleeps above my room. There is no one else, and no sound could alarm those who are in the farther wing.

'Sir Eustace retired about half-past ten. The servants had already gone to their quarters. I sat until after eleven in this room, absorbed in a book. Then I walked round to see that all was right before I went upstairs. Customarily, I went into each of the rooms, and finally the dining-room. As I approached the French window, I suddenly found myself face to face with a broad-shouldered elderly man, who had just stepped into the room. Behind the first man, I saw two others in the light of my candle, who were in the act of entering. I stepped back, but the fellow caught me, first by the wrist, and then by the throat. I opened my mouth to scream, but he struck me a savage blow with his fist over the eye, and I fell on the ground. I must have been unconscious for a few minutes, for when I came to myself, I found that they had torn down the bell rope, and had secured me tightly to the oaken chair in the dining table, with a hankerchief stuffed in my mouth. At this instant, my unfortunate husband entered the room. He had evidently heard some suspicious sounds, and came prepared with his a blackthorn cudgel in his hand. He rushed at the burglars, but the elderly man picked the poker and struck him a horrible blow. He fell with a groan and never moved again. I fainted once more, and when I opened my eyes, found that they had collected the silver from the sideboard, and each one had a glass of wine in hand. They appeared to be a father and two sons team, and talked together in whispers. Ensuring I was bound securely, they left through the window. It took me a quarter of an hour to free my mouth, and scream for help. That is really all that I can tell you, gentlemen,'

'Any questions, Mr Holmes?' asked Hopkins.

'I will not impose any further tax upon Lady Brackenstall's patience and time,' said Holmes.

He looked at the maid.

'Before I go into the dining room I should like to hear your experience.'

'As I sat by my bedroom window, I saw three men in the moonlight down by the lodge gate,' the maid said. 'But I thought nothing of it at the time. It was more than an hour after that I heard my mistress scream, and down I ran, to find her, just as she says, and him on the floor, with his blood and brains over the room. It was enough to drive a woman out of her wits, tied there and her very dress spotted with him. You've questioned her long enough, and now she is going to her room, just with her old Theresa, to get the rest that she badly needs.'

'She has been with her all her life,' said Hopkins. 'Theresa Wright is her name. This way, Mr Holmes, if you please!'

By now, I could see from my friend's expressive face that he had lost all interest in this simple case. An enigmatic and learned specialist who finds that he has been called in for a case of measles would experience something of the annoyance which I read in my friend's eyes. Yet the scene in the dining room of the Abbey Grange was strange enough to recall his waning interest.

The large and high chamber had a carved oak ceiling, and a variety of deer's heads and ancient weapons around the walls. At the far was the high French window of which we had heard. Three smaller windows on the right, and a deep fireplace fell on the left. Beside the fireplace was a heavy oaken chair, and in and out through the open woodwork was woven a crimson cord, which was secured at each side to the crosspiece below. In releasing the lady, the cord had been slipped off her, but the knots, with which it had been secured, still remained.

On the tigerskin hearthrug in front of the fire lay the body of a tall, well-built man, about forty years of age. He lay on his back, holding a blackthorn stick in his hands. He wore an embroidered nightshirt, and his head was horribly injured. Beside him lay the heavy poker, bent into a curve by the concussion. Holmes examined both it and the indescribable wreck that it had wrought.

'He must be a powerful man, this elder Randall,' he remarked.

'Yes,' said Hopkins. 'I have some record of the fellow, and he is a rough customer. We have been on the look-out for him, and now that we know that the gang are here, I don't see how they can escape. We have the news at every seaport already, and a reward will be offered before evening. What beats me is how they could have done so mad a thing, knowing that the lady could describe them and that we could not fail to recognize the description.'

'Exactly. One would have expected that they would silence Lady Brackenstall as well.'

'They may not have realized,' I suggested, 'that she had recovered from her faint.'

'That is likely enough. If she seemed to be senseless, they would not take her life. What about this poor fellow, Hopkins?'

'He was a good-hearted man when he was sober, but a perfect fiend when he was drunk. In spite of all his wealth and his title, he very nearly came our way once or twice. There was a scandal about his drenching a dog with petroleum and setting it on fire—her ladyship's dog, to make the matter worse. Then he threw a decanter at that maid, Theresa Wright—there was trouble about that. What are you looking at now?'

Holmes was down on his knees, examining with great attention the knots upon the red cord with which the lady had been secured, carefully scrutinizing the broken and frayed end where it had snapped off when the burglar had dragged it down.

'When this was pulled down, the bell in the kitchen must have rung loudly,' he remarked.

'No one could hear it. The kitchen stands right at the back of the house.'

'How did the burglar know that no one would hear it? How dared he pull at a bell rope in that reckless fashion?'

'Exactly, Mr Holmes, exactly. I've asked this question to myself so many times. There can be no doubt that this fellow must have known the house and its habits. He must have perfectly understood that the servants would all be in bed at that hour, and that no one could possibly hear a bell ring in the kitchen. Therefore, he must have been in close league with one of the servants. But there are eight servants, and all of good character.'

'Other things being equal,' said Holmes, 'one would suspect the one at whose head the master threw a decanter. The lady's story certainly seems to be corroborated, if it needed corroboration, by every detail which we see before us.'

He walked to the French window and threw it open.

'What did they take?'

'Well, they did not take much—only half a dozen articles of plate off the sideboard. Lady Brackenstall thinks that they were themselves so disturbed by the death of Sir Eustace that they did not ransack the house, as they would otherwise have done.'

'No doubt that is true, and yet they drank some wine, I understand.'

The three glasses were grouped together, all of them tinged with wine, and one of them containing some dregs of beeswing. The bottle stood near them, two-thirds full, and beside it lay a long, deeply stained cork.

A change had come over Holmes's manner. He raised the cork and examined it minutely.

'How did they draw it?' he asked.

Hopkins pointed to a half-opened drawer. In it lay some table linen and a large corkscrew.

'That screw was not used. This bottle was opened by a pocket screw, probably contained in a knife, and not more than an inch and a half long. If you will examine the top of the cork, you will observe that the screw was driven in three times before the cork was extracted. It has never been transfixed. This long screw would have transfixed it and drawn it up with a single pull. When you catch this fellow, you will find that he has one of these multiplex knives in his possession.'

'Excellent!' said Hopkins.

'But these glasses do puzzle me, I confess. Lady Brackenstall actually saw the three men drinking, did she not?'

'Yes, she was clear about that.'

'Then there is the end of it. And yet, you must admit, that the three glasses are very remarkable, Hopkins. What? You see nothing remarkable? Well, well, let it pass. Perhaps, when a man has special knowledge and powers like mine, it makes him look at complex explanations rather than simple ones. Well, Hopkins, I don't see that I can be of any use to you, and you appear to have your case very clear. You will let me know when Randall is arrested, and any further developments which may occur. Come, Watson, let us go back home.'

During our return journey, I could gauge by Holmes's expression that he was pre-occupied with an observation.

'Excuse me, my dear fellow,' said he, just as our train was crawling out of a suburban station, springing on to the platform and pulling me out after him.

'I am sorry to make you the victim of what may seem a mere whim, but while the story and all its corroborations sounds sufficient and complete, my instincts tell me something is absurdly wrong.'

'There are details in her story which, if we looked at in cold blood, would excite our suspicion. These burglars made a considerable haul at Sydenham a fortnight ago. Some account of them and of their appearance was in the papers, and would naturally occur to anyone who wished to invent a story in which imaginary robbers should play a part. As a matter of fact, burglars who have done a good stroke of business are, as a rule, only too glad to enjoy the proceeds in peace and quiet without embarking on another perilous undertaking. Again, it is unusual for burglars to operate at so early an hour, it is unusual for burglars to strike a lady to prevent her screaming, since one would imagine that was the sure way to make her scream, it is unusual for them to commit murder when their numbers are sufficient to overpower one man, it is unusual for them to be content with a limited plunder when there was much more within their reach, and finally, I should say, that it was very unusual for such men to leave a bottle half empty. How do all these unusuals strike you, Watson?'

'Their cumulative effect is certainly considerable, and yet each of them is quite possible in itself. The most unusual thing of all, as it seems to me, is that the lady should be tied to the chair.'

'Well, I am not so clear about that, Watson, for it is evident that they must either kill her or else secure her in such a way that she could not give immediate notice of their escape. There is a certain element of improbability about the lady's story. Especially the incident of the wineglasses.'

'What about the wineglasses?'

'We are told that three men drank from them. But there was beeswing only in one glass. What do you make of it?'

'The last glass filled would be most likely to contain beeswing.'

'Not at all. The bottle was full of it, and it is impossible that the first two glasses were clear and the third heavily charged with it. There are two possible explanations. One is that after the second glass was filled the bottle was violently agitated, and so the third glass received the beeswing. That does not appear probable. No, no, I am sure that I am right.'

'What, then, do you suppose?'

'That only two glasses were used, and that the dregs of both were poured into a third glass, so as to give the false impression that three people had been here. And if this is true, it only means that Lady Brackenstall and her maid have deliberately lied to us, that they have some very strong reason for covering the real criminal, and that we must construct our case for ourselves without any help from them. That is the mission which now lies before us, and here, Watson, is the Sydenham train.'

On our return, Sherlock Holmes took possession of the dining room, locked the door upon the inside, and devoted himself for two hours of intense investigations. The window, the curtains, the carpet, the chair, the rope— each in turn was minutely examined and duly pondered. The body of the unfortunate baronet had been removed, and all else remained as we had seen it in the morning. Finally, to my astonishment, Holmes climbed up on to the massive mantelpiece. For a long time he gazed upward at the red cord, which was still attached to the wire, and then, in an attempt to get nearer, he rested his knee upon a wooden bracket on the wall. This brought his hand within a few inches of the broken end of the rope, but it was not this so much as the bracket itself which seemed to engage his attention. Finally, he sprang down with an ejaculation of satisfaction.

'We have got our case, Watson,' said he.

'You have got your men?'

'Man, Watson, man. Six foot three in height, active as a squirrel, dexterous with his fingers, finally, remarkably quick-witted, for this whole ingenious story is of his concoction. And yet, in that bell rope, he has given us a clue which should not have left us a doubt.'

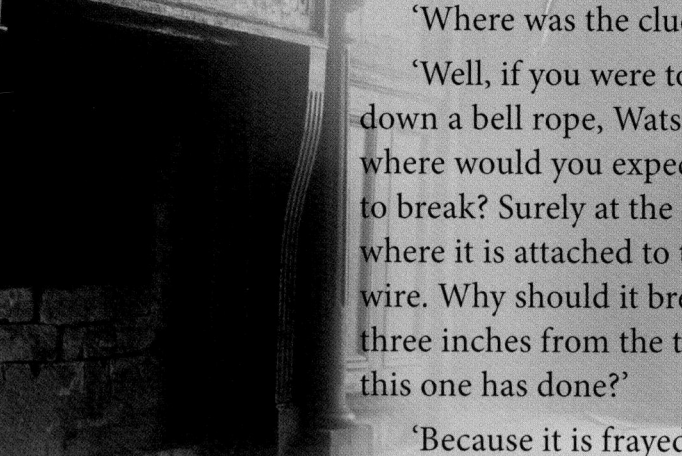

'Where was the clue?'

'Well, if you were to pull down a bell rope, Watson, where would you expect it to break? Surely at the spot where it is attached to the wire. Why should it break three inches from the top, as this one has done?'

'Because it is frayed there?'

'Exactly. This end, which we can examine, is frayed. But the other end is not. If you were on the mantelpiece you would see that it is cut clean off without any mark of fraying whatever. You can reconstruct what occurred. The man needed the rope, but wouldn't tear it down for fear of giving the alarm by ringing the bell. So he sprang up on the mantelpiece, could not quite reach it, put his knee on the bracket—you will see the impression in the dust—and so got his knife to bear upon the cord. I could not reach the place by at least three inches—from which I infer that he is at least three inches a bigger man than I. Look at that mark upon the seat of the oaken chair! What is it?'

'Blood.'

'Undoubtedly it is blood. This alone puts the lady's story out of court. If she were seated on the chair when the crime was done, there wouldn't have been any mark. She was placed in the chair after the death of her husband. I should like now to have a few words with the nurse, Theresa.'

The stern Australian nurse did not attempt to conceal her hatred for her late employer.

'Yes, sir, it is true that he threw the decanter at me. I heard him call my mistress a name, and I told him that he would not dare to speak so if her brother had been there. Then it was that he threw it at me. He was forever ill-treating her, and she, too proud to complain. She never told me of those marks on her arm that you saw this morning, but I know very well that they come from a stab with a hatpin. The sly devil—a devil he was, if ever one walked the earth. He was all honey when first we met him—only eighteen months ago, when she had only just arrived in London. Yes, it was her first voyage—she had never been from home before. He won her with his title and his money and his false London ways. We arrived in June, and they were married in January of last year. She is in the morning-room again, but you must not ask too much of her, for she has gone through all that flesh and blood will stand.'

Lady Brackenstall was reclining on the same couch, but looked brighter than before.

'I hope,' said the lady, 'that you have not come to cross-examine me again?'

'I will not cause you any unnecessary trouble, Lady Brackenstall, and my whole desire is to make things easy for you, for I am convinced that you are a much-tried woman. If you will treat me as a friend and trust me, you may find that I will justify your trust.'

'What do you want me to do?'

'To tell me the truth.'

'You are an impudent fellow!' cried Theresa. 'Do you mean to say that my mistress has told a lie?'

'Have you nothing to tell me?' asked Holmes.

For an instant there was hesitation in her beautiful face. Then some new strong thought caused it to set like a mask.

'I have told you all I know.'

'I am sorry,' he said, and without another word we left the room and the house. There was a frozen pond in the park, but a single hole was left for the convenience of a solitary swan. Holmes gazed at it, and then passed on to the lodge gate. There he scribbled a short note for Stanley Hopkins, and left it with the lodge-keeper.

'I think our next scene of operations must be the shipping office of the Adelaide-Southampton line.'

Holmes's card sent in to the manager ensured instant attention, and he was not long in acquiring all the information he needed. In June of 1895, only one of their line had reached a home port. It was the *Rock of Gibraltar*, their largest and best boat. A reference to the passenger list showed that Miss Fraser, of Adelaide, with her maid had made the voyage in her. Her officers were the same as in 1895, with one exception. The first officer, Mr Jack Crocker, had been made a captain and was to take charge of their new ship, the *Bass Rock*, sailing in two days' time from Southampton.

His record was magnificent, and his character without a mark. We left the office of the Adelaide-Southampton company with this information and drove to Scotland Yard. Instead of entering, Holmes sat in his cab, lost in profound thought. Finally he drove round to the Charing Cross telegraph office, sent off a message, and then, at last, we made for Baker Street once more.

'No, I couldn't do it, Watson,' said he, as we reentered our room. 'Once or twice in my career I feel that I have done more real harm by my discovery of the criminal than ever he had done by his crime. I have learned caution now, and I had rather play tricks with the law of England than with my own conscience. Let us know a little more before we act.'

Before evening, we had a visit from Inspector Stanley Hopkins.

'I believe that you are a wizard, Mr Holmes. How could you know that the stolen silver was at the bottom of that pond? You have made this simple affair far more difficult. What sort of burglars are they who steal silver and then throw it into the nearest pond?'

'I was merely going on the idea that if the silver had been taken by persons who did not want it—who merely took it for a blind, as it were—then they would naturally be anxious to get rid of it.'

'But why should such an idea cross your mind?'

'Well, I thought it was possible. When they came out through the French window, there was the pond with one tempting little hole in the ice, right in front of their noses. Could there be a better hiding-place?'

'Ah, a hiding-place—that is better!' cried Stanley Hopkins. 'It was early, there were folk upon the roads, they were afraid of being seen with the silver, so they sank it in the pond, intending to

return for it when the coast was clear. Excellent, Mr Holmes—that is better than your idea of a blind. But I have had a bad setback—the Randall gang were arrested in New York this morning.'

'Dear me, Hopkins! That is certainly rather against your theory that they committed a murder in Kent last night.'

'It is fatal, Mr Holmes—absolutely fatal. I have got to get to the bottom of the business. I suppose you have no hint to give me?'

'I have given you one.'

'Which?'

'Well, I suggested a blind. But I commend the idea to your mind. Well, goodbye, and let us know how you get on.'

Dinner was over, and the table cleared when there was a sound upon the stairs, and our door was opened to admit a fine, tall young man.

'Sit down, Captain Crocker. You got my telegram?'

Our visitor sank into an armchair and looked from one to the other of us with questioning eyes.

'I got your telegram, and I came at the hour you said. I heard that you had been down to the office. There was no getting away from you. What are you going to do with me? Arrest me?'

'I should not sit here smoking with you if I thought that you were a common criminal,' said Holmes. 'Be frank with me and give me a true account of all that happened at the Abbey Grange last night—a *true* account, mind you, with nothing added and nothing taken off. I know so much already that if you go one inch off the straight, I'll blow this police whistle from my window and the affair goes out of my hands forever.'

The sailor thought for a little.

'I'll chance it,' he cried. 'I believe you are a man of your word, but one thing I will say first. I regret nothing and would do it all again and be proud of the job. Damn the beast, but it's the lady that I care about, and would give my life just to bring one smile to her dear face.

'You seem to know everything, so I expect that you know that I met her when she was a passenger and I was first officer of the *Rock of Gibraltar*. From the first day I met her, she was the only woman to me. Every day of that voyage I loved her more, and she treated me as fairly as ever a woman treated a man. It was all love on my side, and all good comradeship and friendship on hers. Next time I came back from sea, I heard of her marriage. I didn't grieve over her marriage, and rejoiced that good luck had come her way.

'I never thought to see her again, but last voyage I was promoted, and had to wait for a couple of months at Sydenham for the new boat. One day out in a country lane I met Theresa Wright, her old maid who told me everything. I tell you, gentlemen, it nearly drove me mad. Then I met Mary herself—and met her again. Then she would meet me no more. I had a notice that I was to start on my voyage within a week, and I determined that I would see her once before I left.

'I learned the ways of the house from Theresa and crept to the room last night where Mary sat reading. At first she would not open to me, but then whispered to me to come round to the big front window, to let me into the dining room. I was standing with her just inside the window, in all innocence, as God is my judge, when he rushed like a madman into the room, called her the vilest name that a man could use to a woman, and welted her across the face with the stick he had in his hand. I had sprung for the poker, and it was a fair fight between us. Do you think I was sorry? Not I! It was his life or mine, but far more than that, it was his life or hers, for how could I leave her in the power of this madman? That was how I killed him. Was I wrong? Well, then, what would either of you gentlemen have done, if you had been in my position?

'She had screamed when he struck her, and that brought old Theresa down from the room above. There was a bottle of wine on the sideboard, and I opened it and poured a little between Mary's lips, for she was half dead with shock. Theresa was as cool as ice, and it was her plot as much as mine. We must make it appear that burglars had done the thing. Theresa kept on repeating our story to her mistress, while I swarmed up and cut the rope of the bell. Then I lashed her in her chair, and frayed out the end of the rope to make it look natural. I gathered up a few plates and pots of silver, to carry out the idea of the robbery, and there I left them, with orders to give the alarm when I had a quarter of an hour's start. I dropped the silver into the pond, and made off for Sydenham. And that's the truth and the whole truth, Mr Holmes, if it costs me my neck.'

'That's what I think,' said Holmes. 'I know that every word is true. No one but an acrobat or a sailor could have got up to that bell rope from the bracket, and no one but a sailor could have made the knots with which the cord was fastened to the chair.'

'I thought the police never could have seen through our dodge.'

'And the police haven't, nor will they, to the best of my belief. Now, look here, Captain Crocker, this is a very serious matter, and I am not sure that in defense of your own life your action will not be pronounced legitimate. However, that is for a British jury to decide.

Meanwhile if you choose to disappear in the next twenty-four hours, I will promise you that no one will hinder you.'

'And then it will all come out?'

'Certainly.'

The sailor flushed with anger.

'Do you think I would leave Mary alone to face the music while I slunk away? No, sir, let them do their worst upon me, but for heaven's sake, Mr Holmes, find some way of keeping my poor Mary out of the courts.'

'I was only testing you, and you ring true every time. I have given Hopkins an excellent hint and if he can't avail himself of it I can do no more. See here, Captain Crocker, we'll do this in due form of law. You are the prisoner. Watson, you are a British jury, and I never met a man who was more eminently fitted to represent one. I am the judge. Now, gentleman of the jury, you have heard the evidence. Do you find the prisoner guilty or not guilty?'

'Not guilty, my lord,' said I.

'Then so be it. You are acquitted, Captain Crocker. So long as the law does not find some other victim you are safe from me. Come back to this lady in a year, and may her future and yours justify us in the judgment which we have pronounced this night!'

The Adventure of the Dancing Men

of the

Dancing Men

Arthur Conan Doyle

Holmes had been sitting quietly with his long, thin back curved over a chemical vessel, brewing a foul smelling product, when he suddenly tossed a sheet of paper upon the table, and said, 'Here is an unexplained problem, friend Watson. See what you can make of that.'

I examined the absurd hieroglyphics on the paper with amazement.

'Why, Holmes, it is a child's drawing. What else should it be?' I asked.

'That is what Mr Hilton Cubitt, of Riding Thorpe Manor, Norfolk, is anxious to know. This confusing drawing came by post, and he was to follow by the next train. There's a ring at the bell, and I wouldn't be surprised if it were him.'

An instant later, a tall, clean-shaven gentleman, with clear eyes and florid cheeks, entered the room. He seemed to bring a whiff of his strong, fresh, east-coast air with him. Having shaken hands with us, he was about to sit down, when his eye rested upon the paper with the curious markings kept on the table.

'Well, Mr Holmes, what do you make of these?' he asked.

'It is certainly rather a curious production,' said Holmes. 'At first sight it would appear to be some

childish prank. It consists of a number of absurd little figures dancing across the paper upon which they are drawn. Why should you attribute any importance to so grotesque an object?'

It was a page torn from a notebook, with markings done in pencil.

'I never should, Mr Holmes. But my wife does. It is frightening her to death. She says nothing, but I can see terror in her eyes. That's why I want to sift the matter to the bottom.'

Holmes examined it for some time, and then, folding it carefully up, he placed it in his pocketbook.

'This promises to be a most interesting and unusual case,' said he. 'You gave me a few particulars in your letter, Mr Hilton Cubitt, but could you kindly go over it all again for the benefit of my friend, Dr Watson.'

'I'm not much of a story-teller,' said our visitor nervously. 'I'll begin at the time of my marriage last year, but I want to say first of all that, though I'm not a rich man, my people have been at Riding Thorpe for a matter of five centuries, and there is no better known family in the County of Norfolk. Last year I came up to London for the Jubilee, and I stopped at a boarding house in Russell Square, because Parker, the vicar of our

parish, was staying in it. I became friends with an American young lady— Elsie Patrick there, and within a month, I was as much in love with her as man could be. We were quietly married at a registry office, and we returned to Norfolk a wedded couple. You'll think it very mad, Mr Holmes, that a man of a good old family should marry a wife in this fashion, knowing nothing of her past or of her people, but if you saw her and knew her, it would help you to understand.

'She was very straight about it, was Elsie. I can't say that she did not give me every chance of getting out of it if I wished to do so. "I have had some very disagreeable associations in

my life," said she, "I would rather never allude
to the past, for it is very painful to me. If you
take me, Hilton, you will take a woman who has
nothing that she need be personally ashamed of,
but you will have to be content with my word for
it, and to allow me to be silent as to all that passed
up to the time when I became yours. If these
conditions are too hard, then go back to Norfolk,
and leave me to the lonely life in which you
found me."

'It was the day before our wedding that she
said those very words to me. I told her that I was
content to take her on her own terms, and I have
been as good as my word.

'We have been married happily now for a
year, but about a month ago, at the end of June,
I saw the first signs of trouble. One day my wife
received a letter from America—turned deadly
white reading it, and threw it into the fire. She
made no allusion to it afterwards, and I made
none, for a promise is a promise, but she has
never known an easy hour from that moment.
There is always a look of fear upon her face, but
until she speaks, I can say nothing. Mind you, she
is a truthful woman, Mr Holmes, and would never
bring any stain upon my family honour—of that
I am sure.

'Last Tuesday, I found on one of the window-sills a number of absurd little dancing figures like these upon the paper. They were scrawled with chalk. I thought that it was the stable boy who had drawn them, but the lad swore he knew nothing about it. I had them washed out, and only mentioned the matter to my wife afterwards. To my surprise, she took it very seriously, and begged me if any more came to let her see them. None did come for a week, and then yesterday morning I found this paper lying on the sundial in the garden. I showed it to Elsie, and down she dropped in a dead faint. Since then she has looked like a woman in a dream, half dazed, and with terror always lurking in her eyes. It was then that I wrote and sent the paper to you, Mr Holmes. It was not a thing that I could take to the police, for they would have laughed at me, but you will tell me what to do. I am not a rich man, but if there is any danger threatening my little woman, I would spend my last copper to shield her.'

'Don't you think that your best plan would be to make a direct appeal to your wife, and to ask her to share her secret with you?' Holmes asked Mr Cubitt.

'A promise is a promise, Mr Holmes. If Elsie wished to tell me she would. If not, it is not for me to force her confidence. But I am justified in taking my own line—and I will.'

'Then I will help you with all my heart. These hieroglyphics have evidently a meaning. If it is a purely arbitrary one, it may be impossible for us to solve it. If, on the other hand, it is systematic, I have no doubt that we shall get to the bottom of it. But this particular sample is so short, and the facts that you have brought are so indefinite that we have no basis for an investigation. I would suggest that you return to Norfolk and keep a keen lookout, and take an exact copy of any fresh dancing men which may appear. Make a discreet enquiry also as to any strangers in the neighbourhood. When you have collected some fresh evidence, come to me again. If there are any fresh developments, I shall be ready to see you in your Norfolk home.'

Over the next few days, I saw Holmes buried deep in thought, examining the slip of paper and the curious figures upon it. About a fortnight or so later, I was going out when he called me back.

'You remember Hilton Cubbit, of the dancing men? He may be here any moment. I gather from his wire that there have been some new incidents of importance.'

We didn't have to wait long, as Mr Cubbit came straight from the station. He looked worried and depressed.

'It's getting on my nerves, this business, Mr Holmes,' said he, as he sank into an armchair. 'It's bad enough to feel that you are surrounded by unknown folk, but when, in addition to that, you know that it is just killing your wife by inches, it becomes as much as flesh and blood can endure.'

'But have you found out something?'

'A good deal, Mr Holmes. I have several fresh dancing men pictures for you to examine, and, more importantly, I have seen the fellow.'

'What, the man who draws them?'

'Yes, I saw him at his work. But I will tell you everything in order. When I got back after my visit to you, the very first thing I saw next morning, was a fresh crop of dancing men. They had been drawn in chalk upon the black wooden door of the tool-house. I took an exact copy, and here it is.'

He unfolded a paper and laid it upon the table.

'I rubbed out the marks, but, two morning later, a fresh inscription had appeared, and have got a copy of it here.'

Holmes rubbed his hands and chuckled with delight.

'Our material is rapidly accumulating,' said he.

'Three days later a message was left scrawled upon paper, placed upon the sundial. Here it is. The characters were exactly the same as the last one. After that I determined to lie in wait, so I got out my revolver and I sat up in my study, which overlooks the lawn and garden. About two in the morning I was seated by the window, when I heard steps behind me, and there was my wife imploring me to come to bed. I told her that I wished to see who it was who played such absurd tricks upon us. She answered that it was some senseless practical joke, and that I should not take any notice of it.

'Suddenly, as she spoke, I saw a dark, creeping figure which crawled round the corner and squatted in front of the door. Seizing my pistol,

I was rushing out, when my wife threw her arms round me and held me with convulsive strength. At last I got clear, but by the time I had opened the door and reached the house the creature was gone. He had left a trace of his presence, however, for there on the door was the very same arrangement of dancing men which had already twice appeared, and which I have copied on that paper. There was no other sign of the fellow anywhere, and yet when I examined the door again in the morning, he had scrawled some more of his pictures under the line which I had already seen. It's very short, but I made a copy of it.'

Again he produced a paper.

'Excellent! This is far the most important of all for our purpose. It fills me with hopes. Now, Mr Hilton Cubitt, please continue.'

'I have nothing more to say, Mr Holmes, except that I was angry with my wife that night for holding me back. She said that she feared that I might come to harm. For an instant it had crossed my mind that perhaps what she really feared was that he might come to harm, for I could not doubt that she knew who this man was, and what he meant by these strange signals. But there is a tone in my wife's voice, Mr Holmes, and a look in her eyes which forbid doubt, and I am sure that it was indeed my own safety that was in her mind. There's the whole case, and now I want your advice as to what I ought to do.'

'Leave me these papers, and I think that it is very likely that I shall be able to pay you a visit shortly and to throw some light upon your case.'

Sherlock Holmes preserved his calm professional manner until our visitor had left us, but it was easy for me to see his profound excitement. The moment Hilton Cubitt disappeared through the door, my comrade rushed to the table, laid out all the slips of paper containing dancing men in front of him, and threw himself into an intricate and elaborate calculation. The next couple of hours were spent in deciphering the hidden codes. Finally, he sprang from his chair with a cry of satisfaction, and walked up and down the room rubbing his hands together. Then he wrote a long telegram upon a cable form.

'If my answer to this is as I hope, you will have a very pretty case to add to your collection, Watson,' said he. 'I expect that we shall be able to go down to Norfolk tomorrow, and to take our friend some very definite news as to the secret of his annoyance.'

After two days of impatient waiting, there came a letter from Hilton Cubitt, along with another drawing of the dancing men that was found that morning on the sundial.

Holmes bent over this grotesque frieze for some minutes, and then suddenly sprang to his feet with an exclamation of surprise and dismay. His face was haggard with anxiety.

'We have let this affair go far enough,' said he. 'We have to take the very first train in the morning to North Walsham. Our presence is most urgently needed. Ah! Here is our expected cablegram. This message makes it even more essential that we should not lose an hour in letting Hilton Cubitt know how matters stand, for it is a singular and a dangerous web in which our simple Norfolk squire is entangled.'

We had hardly alighted at North Walsham, and mentioned the name of our destination, when the station master hurried towards us. 'I suppose

that you are the detectives from London?' asked he.

'What makes you think such a thing?' asked Holmes, a bit annoyed.

'Because Inspector Martin from Norwich has just passed through. But maybe you are the surgeons. She's not dead—or wasn't by last accounts. You may be in time to save her yet—though it be for the gallows.'

Holmes's brow was dark with anxiety.

'We are going to Riding Thorpe Manor,' said he, 'but we have heard nothing of what has passed there.'

'It's a terrible business,' said the station master. 'They are shot, both Mr Hilton Cubitt and his wife. She shot him and then herself—so the servants say. He's dead and she is in danger.

Dear, dear, one of the oldest families in the county of Norfolk, and one of the most honoured.'

Holmes hurried to the carriage, and never spoke once during the seven miles' drive. He had been uneasy all through our journey from town, but now this sudden realization of his worst fears left him in a blank melancholy.

As we drove up to the porticoed front door of the Riding Thorpe Manor, I observed that a dapper little man, with an alert manner and a waxed moustache, had descended from a high dog-cart. He introduced himself as Inspector Martin, of the Norfolk Constabulary, and he was considerably astonished when he heard the name of my companion.

'Why, Mr Holmes, the crime was only committed at three this morning. How could you hear of it in London and get to the spot as soon as I?'

'I anticipated it. I came in the hope of preventing it.'

'Then you must have important evidence, of which we are ignorant, for they were said to be a most united couple.'

'I have only the evidence of the dancing men,' said Holmes. 'Since it is too late to prevent this tragedy, I am very anxious that I should use the knowledge which I possess in order to insure that justice be done. Will you associate me in your investigation, or will you prefer that I should act independently?'

'I should be proud to feel that we were acting together, Mr Holmes,' said the inspector, earnestly.

'In that case I should be glad to hear the evidence and to examine the premises without an instant of unnecessary delay.'

Inspector Martin had the good sense to allow my friend to do things in his own fashion, and contented himself with carefully noting the results. The local surgeon, an old, white-haired man, had just come down from Mrs Hilton Cubitt's room, and he reported that her injuries were serious, but not necessarily fatal. The bullet had passed through the front of her brain, and it would probably be some time before she could

regain consciousness. On the question of whether she had been shot or had shot herself, he would not venture to express any decided opinion. Certainly the bullet had been discharged at very close quarters. There was only the one pistol found in the room, two barrels of which had been emptied. Mr Hilton Cubitt had been shot through the heart. It was equally conceivable that he had shot her and then himself, or that she had been the criminal, for the revolver lay upon the floor midway between them.

'Has he been moved?' asked Holmes.

'We have moved nothing except the lady. We could not leave her lying wounded upon the floor.'

'And you have touched nothing?'

'Nothing.'

'You have acted with great discretion. Who sent for you?'

'The housemaid, Saunders.'

'Was it she who gave the alarm?'

'She and Mrs King, the cook.'

'Where are they now?'

'In the kitchen, I believe.'

'Then I think we had better hear their story at once.'

The two women told their story clearly enough. They had been aroused from their sleep by the sound of an explosion, which had been followed a minute later by a second one. Together they had descended the stairs. The door of the study was open, and a candle was burning upon the table. Their master lay upon his face in the centre of the room. He was quite dead. Near the window his wife was crouching. She was horribly wounded, and breathed heavily, incapable of saying anything. The passage, as well as the room, was full of smoke and the smell of powder. The window was certainly shut and fastened upon the inside. Both women were positive upon the point. They had at once sent for the doctor and for the constable. Then, with the aid of the groom and the stable boy, they had conveyed their injured mistress to her room. She was clad in her dress—he in his dressing gown, over his night clothes. Nothing had been moved in the study. So far as they knew, there had never been any quarrel between husband and wife and appeared to be a united couple.

These were the main points of the servants' evidence.

'I think we now are in a position to undertake a thorough examination of the room,' said Holmes to his professional colleague.

The study proved to be a small chamber, lined on three sides with books, and with a writing table facing a window, which looked out upon the garden. Our first attention was given to the body of the unfortunate squire, lying stretched across the room. His disordered dress showed that he had been hastily aroused from sleep. The bullet had been fired at him from the front, and had remained in his body, after penetrating the heart. His death had certainly been instantaneous and painless. There was no powder marking either upon his dressing gown or on his hands. According to the country surgeon, the lady had stains upon her face, but none upon her hand.

'The absence of the latter means nothing, though its presence may mean everything,' said Holmes. 'Unless the powder from a badly fitting cartridge happens to spurt backward, one may fire many shots without leaving a sign. I would suggest that Mr Cubitt's body may now be removed. I suppose, Doctor, you have not recovered the bullet which wounded the lady?'

'A serious operation will be necessary before that can be done. But there are still four cartridges in the revolver. Two have been fired and two wounds inflicted, so that each bullet can be accounted for.'

'Perhaps you can account also for the bullet which has so obviously struck the edge of the window?' said Holmes.

He had turned suddenly, and was pointing to a hole which had been drilled right through the lower window-sash, about an inch above the bottom.

'You are certainly right, sir,' said the country doctor. 'A third shot has been fired, and therefore a third person must have been present. But who could that have been, and how could he have got away?'

'At the time of the firing, the window as well as the door of the room had been open. Otherwise the fumes of powder could not have been blown so rapidly through the house. But they were only open for a very short time, however, because the candle was not guttered. Feeling sure, I conceived that there might have been a third person in the affair, who stood outside this opening and fired through it. Any shot directed at this person might hit the sash. I looked, and there, sure enough, was the bullet mark!'

'But how come the window was shut and fastened?'

'The woman's first instinct would be to shut and fasten the window. But, halloa! What is this?'

It was a lady's hand bag which stood upon the study table and contained twenty fifty-pound notes, held together by an India rubber band.

'This must be preserved, for it will figure in the trial,' said Holmes, as he handed the bag with its contents to the inspector. 'It is now necessary that we should try to throw some light upon this third bullet, which has clearly, from the splintering of the wood, been fired from inside the room. I should like to see Mrs King, the cook, again. You said, Mrs King, that you were awakened by a loud explosion. You don't think that it might have been two shots fired almost at the same instant?'

'I am sure I couldn't say, sir.'

'I believe that it was undoubtedly so. Inspector Martin, if you will kindly step round with me, we shall see what evidence the garden has to offer.'

The flowers were trampled down, and the soft soil was imprinted all over with footmarks. Large, masculine feet they were, with peculiarly long, sharp toes. Holmes hunted about among the grass and leaves like a retriever after a wounded bird. Then, with a cry of satisfaction, he bent forward and picked up a little brazen cylinder.

'I thought so,' said he, 'the revolver had an ejector, and here is the third cartridge. I really

think, Inspector Martin, that our case is almost complete.'

'Whom do you suspect?' he asked.

'I'll go into that later. First of all, I wish to know whether there is any inn in this neighbourhood known as "Elrige's"?'

The stable boy threw a light upon the matter by remembering that a farmer of that name lived some miles off, in the direction of East Ruston.

He took from his pocket the various slips of the dancing men. With these in front of him, he worked for some time at the study table. Finally he handed a note to the boy, with directions to put it into the hands of the person to whom it was addressed, and especially to answer no questions of any sort which might be put to him. I saw the outside of the note, addressed in straggling, irregular characters, very unlike Holmes's usual precise hand. It was consigned to 'Mr Abe Slaney, Elriges Farm, East Ruston, Norfolk'.

'I think, Inspector,' Holmes remarked, 'that you would do well to telegraph for an escort, as, if my calculations prove to be correct, you may have a particularly dangerous prisoner to convey to the county jail. The boy who takes this note could no doubt forward your telegram. If there is an afternoon train to town, Watson, I think we

should take it, as this investigation draws rapidly to a close.'

When the youth had been dispatched, Holmes instructed the servants that if any visitor were to call asking for Mrs Hilton Cubitt, no information should be given as to her condition, but he was to be shown at once into the drawing room.

'I think that I can help you to pass an hour in an interesting and profitable manner,' said Holmes, drawing his chair up to the table, and spreading out in front of him the various papers upon which were recorded the antics of the dancing men. He then explained in great detail how he had decoded the secret language to decipher what the codes meant. Through tracking each alphabet, Holmes reached the conclusion that the messages were being sent by a certain Abe Slaney.

'I had every reason to suppose that this Abe Slaney was an American, since Abe is an American contraction, and since a letter from America had been the starting point of all the trouble. I had also every cause to think that there was some criminal secret in the matter. The lady's allusions to her past, and her refusal to take her husband into her confidence, both pointed in that direction. I therefore cabled to my friend, Wilson Hargreave, of the New York Police Bureau and asked him whether the name of Abe Slaney was known to him. Here is his reply: "The most dangerous crook in Chicago". Another message decoded and I realized that the rascal was on his way to commit something heinous. I at once came to Norfolk with my friend and colleague, Dr Watson, but, unhappily, only in time to find that the worst had already occurred.'

'If this Abe Slaney, living at Elrige's, is indeed the murderer, and if he has made his escape while I am seated here, I should certainly get into serious trouble,' said the inspector.

'You need not be uneasy. He will not try to escape because I have asked him to come here.'

'But this is incredible, Mr Holmes! Why should

he come because you have asked him? Would not such a request rather rouse his suspicions and cause him to fly?'

'I think I have known how to frame the letter,' said Sherlock Holmes. 'In fact, if I am not very much mistaken, here is the gentleman himself coming up the drive.'

A man was striding up the path which led to the door. We waited in silence for a minute—one of those minutes which one can never forget. Then the door opened and the man stepped in. In an instant Holmes clapped a pistol to his head, and Martin slipped the handcuffs over his wrists. It was all done so swiftly and deftly that the fellow was helpless before he knew that he was attacked.

'I have nothing to hide from you, gentlemen,' said he. 'If I shot the man he had his shot at me, and there's no murder in that. But if you think I could have hurt that woman, then you don't know either me or her.'

'She broke away from your influence when she found the man that you are,' said Holmes, sternly. 'She fled from America to avoid you, and she married an honourable gentleman in England. You dogged her and followed her and made her life a misery to her, in order to induce her to abandon the husband whom she loved and respected in order to fly with you, whom she feared and hated. You have ended by bringing about the death of a noble man and driving his wife to suicide. That is your record in this business, Mr Abe Slaney, and you will answer for it to the law.'

'If Elsie dies, I care nothing what becomes of me,' said the American.

He opened one of his hands, and looked at a note crumpled up in his palm.

'See here, mister!' he cried, with a gleam of suspicion in his eyes, 'you're not trying to scare me over this, are you? If the lady is hurt as bad as you say, who was it that wrote this note?'

He tossed it forward on to the table.

'I wrote it, to bring you here.'

'How came you to write it?'

'What one man can invent another can discover,' said Holmes. 'There is a cab coming to convey you to Norwich, Mr Slaney. But

meanwhile, you have time to make some amends for the injury you have caused.'

'First of all, I want you gentlemen to understand that I have known this lady since she was a child,' said Slaney. 'There were seven of us in a gang in Chicago, and Elsie's father was the boss of the Joint. He was a clever man, was old Patrick. It was he who invented that writing, which would pass as a child's scrawl unless you just happened to have the key to it. Well, Elsie learned some of our ways, but she couldn't stand the business, and she had a bit of honest money of her own, so she gave us all the slip and got away to London. She had been engaged to me, and she would have married me, I believe, if I had taken over another profession, but she would have nothing to do with anything on the cross. It was only after her marriage to this Englishman that I was able to find out where she was. I wrote to her, but got no answer. After that I came over, and, as letters were no use, I put my messages where she could read them.

'I have been here a month now. I lived in that farm and tried all I could to coax Elsie away. I knew that she read the messages, for once she wrote an answer under one of them. Then

my temper got the better of me, and I began to
threaten her. She sent me a letter then, asking me
to go away, and saying that it would break her heart
if any scandal should come upon her husband. She
said that she would come down when her husband
was asleep at three in the morning, and speak with
me through the end window, if I would go away
afterwards and leave her in peace. She came down
and brought money with her, trying to bribe me
to go. This made me mad, and I caught her arm
and tried to pull her through the window. At that
moment in rushed the husband with his revolver
in his hand. Elsie had sunk down upon the floor,
and we were face to face. I was heeled also, and
I held up my gun to scare him off and let me get
away. He fired and missed me. I pulled off almost
at the same instant, and down he dropped. I made
away across the garden, and as I went I heard
the window shut behind me. That's God's truth,
gentlemen, every word of it, and I heard no more

about it until that lad came riding up with a note which made me walk in here, like a jay, and give myself into your hands.'

A cab had driven up whilst the American had been talking. Two uniformed policemen sat inside. Inspector Martin rose and touched his prisoner on the shoulder.

We stood at the window and watched the cab drive away. As I turned back, my eye caught the pellet of paper which the prisoner had tossed upon the table.

'If you use the code which I have explained,' said Holmes, 'you will find that it simply means "Come here at once". I was convinced that it was an invitation which he would not refuse, since he could never imagine that it could come from anyone but the lady.'

The American, Abe Slaney, was condemned to death at the winter assizes at Norwich, but his penalty was changed to penal servitude in consideration of mitigating circumstances, and the certainty that Hilton Cubitt had fired the first shot. Of Mrs Hilton Cubitt I only know that I have heard she recovered entirely, and that she still remains a widow, devoting her whole life to the care of the poor and to the administration of her husband's estate.

The Adventure of the Golden Pince-nez

of the Golden Pince-nez

Arthur Conan Doyle

It was a wild night towards the close of November. The wind was howling, while the rain beat fiercely against the window. The streets looked deserted. Holmes and I were sitting in silence, when alone cab pulled up at our door.

'What can he want?' I wondered aloud, as a man stepped out of it.

Our midnight visitor was Stanley Hopkins, a young and promising detective.

'It must be something important which has brought you out in such a storm,' said Holmes.

'It is indeed, Mr Holmes. This is about the Yoxley case. I can make neither head nor tail of it. A man is dead but, so far as I can see, no reason on earth why anyone would want to harm him.'

Holmes lit his cigar and leaned back in his chair.

'Tell us about it,' he said.

'I've got my facts pretty clear,' said Stanley Hopkins. 'I just want know what they all mean. The story, as I understand so far, is like this. Some years ago an elderly man called Professor Coram took a country house, Yoxley Old Place. He was an invalid. He remained in his bed half the time. The other half he hobbled round the house with a stick or was pushed about the grounds by the gardener in a bath chair. He was well liked by the few neighbours who met him. He has the reputation of being a very learned man. His household consisted of an elderly housekeeper, Mrs Marker, and a maid, Susan Tarlton. They have been with him since his arrival, and seem to be women of excellent character. The professor is writing a book, and about a year ago, he decided to employ a secretary. The first two that he tried did not work out, but the third, Mr Willoughby Smith, was just what he wanted. He was a very young man straight from the university. He was a decent, quiet, hard-working fellow, with no weak spot in him at all. And yet he was murdered this morning in the professor's study.'

The wind howled and screamed at the windows. Holmes and I drew closer to the fire, while the young inspector laid out his case.

'The household was completely free from outside influences. Weeks would pass before any of them would go past the garden gate. The professor was buried in his work. Young Smith didn't know anybody in the neighbourhood, and lived very much like his employer. The two women had no reason to step out of the house. Mortimer, the gardener, is a man of excellent character. He lives in a cottage at the other end of the garden. Those are the only people that you would find within the grounds of Yoxley Old Place. The gate of the garden is a hundred yards from the main London to Chatham road. It opens with a latch, and anyone can walk in.'

'Now I will give you the evidence of Susan Tarlton. It was between eleven and twelve in the morning. She was hanging some curtains in the upstairs front bedroom. Professor Coram was still in bed. The housekeeper was busy with some work in the back of the house. Willoughby Smith had been in his bedroom, but the maid heard him at that moment go down into the study immediately below her. About a minute later there was a dreadful cry in the room below. At the same instant there was a heavy thud, which shook the old house, and then all was silence. The maid stood scared for a moment, and then ran downstairs. The study door was shut and she opened it. Inside, Mr Willoughby Smith was stretched upon the floor. As she tried to raise him she saw that blood was pouring from the underside of his neck. It was pierced by a very small but very deep wound. The instrument with which the injury had been inflicted lay beside him. It was one of those small sealing-wax knives found on old-fashioned writing tables. It was part of the fittings of the professor's own desk.

'After the maid poured some water over his forehead, Smith opened his eyes for an instant. "The professor," he murmured, "it was she." The maid is certain that those were his exact words. He tried desperately to say something else, and he held his right hand up in the air. Then he fell back dead.

'In the meantime the housekeeper arrived upon the scene, but she was too late to catch Smith's dying words. She hurried to the professor's room and found him sitting up in bed, still in his nightclothes. It was impossible for him to dress without the help of Mortimer, who was to come in at twelve o'clock. The professor says that he heard the distant cry, but that he knows nothing more. His first action was to send Mortimer for the local police. A little later the chief constable sent for me. Nothing was moved before I got there, and strict orders were given that no one should walk upon the paths leading to the house.'

'Well, tell us, what did you make of it?' asked Holmes

'First, Mr Holmes, you must look at this rough plan, which will give you an idea of the position of the professor's study and the various points of the case.'

He unfolded the rough chart.

'Now, if the assassin entered the house, it was definitely by the garden path and the back door. From here there is direct access to the study. Any other way would have been too complicated. The escape route must have also been the same. There are two other exits from the room. One was blocked by Susan as she ran downstairs and the other leads straight to the professor's bedroom. I therefore directed my attention to the garden path. It was saturated with recent rain, and would certainly show any footmarks.'

'I realized that I was dealing with a cautious and expert criminal. No footprints were found on the path. Someone, however, had certainly passed along the grass border that lines the path in order to avoid leaving a track. It could only have been the murderer, since neither the gardener nor anyone else had been there that morning, and the

rain had only begun during the night.'

'These tracks upon the grass, were they coming or going?' asked Holmes.

'It was impossible to say. There was never any outline.'

'A large foot or a small?'

'You could not distinguish.'

Holmes was growing impatient.

'Well, Hopkins, what did you do after you had made certain that you had made certain of nothing?'

'I think I made certain of a lot of things, Mr Holmes. I knew that someone had entered the house cautiously from outside. I next examined the corridor. It is lined with coconut matting and there was no impression of any kind on it. This brought me into the study. The main article here is a large writing table with a fixed bureau. This bureau consists of some drawers and a small cupboard. The drawers, it seems, were always open, and contained nothing of value. The cupboard was locked, but there were no signs that it had been tampered with. The professor assures me that nothing was missing. It is certain that no robbery was committed.'

'There was, of course, this very important piece of evidence which was found in the dead man's right hand.'

From his pocket Stanley Hopkins drew a small paper packet. He unfolded it and disclosed a golden pince-nez, with two broken ends of black silk cord dangling from its end.

'Willoughby Smith had excellent sight,' he added. 'This was definitely snatched from the assassin.'

Sherlock Holmes took the glasses into his hand, and examined them with the utmost attention and interest. He held them on his nose, tried to read through them, went to the window and stared up the street with them, looked at them most minutely in the full light of the lamp, and finally, with a chuckle, wrote a few lines upon a sheet of paper and tossed it across to Stanley Hopkins.

'That's the best I can do for you,' he said.

The astonished detective read the note aloud.

'Wanted, a well-dressed woman of good address. She has a very thick nose, with eyes which are set close upon either side of it. She has a puckered forehead, a peering expression, and probably rounded shoulders. She may have visited an optician at least twice during the last few months. Since her glasses are of remarkable strength, and there are not those many opticians, there should be no difficulty in tracing her.'

Holmes smiled at Hopkin's astonishment.

'I can tell that these glasses belong to a woman from their delicacy, and also, from the last words of the dying man. They are handsomely mounted in solid gold. Their owner is certainly well-dressed. You will find that the clips are too wide for your nose, showing that the lady's nose was very broad at the base. My own face is a narrow one, and yet I find that I cannot get my eyes into the centre, or even near the centre, of these glasses. Therefore, the lady's eyes are set very near to the sides of the nose. The glasses are concave and of unusual strength. A lady whose vision has been so extremely contracted all her life is sure to have the physical characteristics of such vision, which are seen in the forehead, the eyelids, and the shoulders.'

'But how can you be so sure about the double visit to the optician?' I asked

'You will see,' he said, 'that the clips are lined with tiny bands of cork to soften the pressure upon the nose. One of these is discoloured and slightly worn out, but the other is new. Evidently one has fallen off and been replaced. I would say that the older one has been there for only a few months. They exactly correspond, so I gather that the lady went back to the same place for the second.'

'It's marvellous!' cried Hopkins. 'To think that I had all that evidence in my hand and never knew it! What beats me, however, is the utter lack of a motive to the crime.'

'Ah! I can't help you there. But I suppose you want us to come out tomorrow?'

'If it is not asking too much, Mr Holmes.'

'Your case is certainly very interesting, Hopkins. I shall be delighted to look into it. Well, it's nearly one, and we should get some sleep.'

It was a bitter morning when we started our journey the next day. After a long and tiring train ride, we got off at a small station some miles from Chatham. We had a quick breakfast and were all ready for business when we arrived at Yoxley Old Place. A constable met us at the garden gate.

'This is the garden path of which I spoke, Mr Holmes. There was no mark on it yesterday.'

'On which side were the marks on the grass?'

'This side, sir. This narrow margin of grass between the path and the flower bed.'

'Yes, yes, someone has passed along,' said Holmes, stooping over the grass border. 'Our lady must have been very careful, since on the one side she would have left a track on the path, and on the other an even clearer one on the soft bed. You think she came back this way?'

'Yes, sir.'

'On this strip of grass?'

'Certainly, Mr Holmes.'

'Hum! It was a very remarkable performance. The idea of murder was not in her mind, or she would have carried a weapon, instead of having to pick this knife off the table. She moved along this corridor, leaving no traces upon the coconut matting. Then she found herself in this study. How long was she there?'

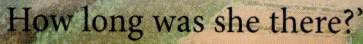

'Not more than a few minutes, sir. Mrs Marker, the housekeeper, had been in there tidying not very long before — about a quarter of an hour, she says.'

'So our lady enters this room, and goes over to the writing table. If there had been anything worthwhile in the drawers, they would surely have been locked up. She was going for something in that wooden bureau. Halloa! What is that scratch? Just hold a match, Watson. Why did you not tell me about this, Hopkins?'

This mark began upon the brass-work on the right-hand side of the keyhole, and extended for about four inches, where it had scratched the varnish from the surface.

'I noticed it, Mr Holmes, but you'll always find scratches round a keyhole.'

'This is quite recent. See how the brass shines where it is cut. An old scratch would be the same colour as the surface. Look at it through my lens. There's the varnish, too, like earth on each side of a furrow. Is Mrs Marker there?'

An elderly woman came into the room.

'Did you dust this bureau yesterday morning?'

'Yes, sir.'

'Did you notice this scratch?'

'No, sir, I did not.'

'I am sure you did not. A duster would have swept away these shreds of varnish. Who has the key of this bureau?'

'The professor keeps it on his watch chain.'

'Is it a simple key?'

'No, sir, it is a Chubb's key.'

'Very good. Mrs Marker, you can go. Now we are making a little progress. Our lady enters the room, advances to the bureau, and either opens it or tries to do so. Meanwhile Willoughby Smith enters the room. In her hurry to withdraw the key, she makes this scratch. He seizes her. She snatches up the nearest object, which happens to be this knife, and strikes at him to make him let go. The blow is fatal. He falls and she escapes, either with or without the object for which she has come. Is Susan, the maid, there? Could anyone have got away through that door after the time that you heard the cry, Susan?'

'No sir, it is impossible. I'd have seen anyone in the passage.'

'This other passage leads only to the professor's room. There is no exit that way?'

'No, sir.'

'Let's go down it and meet the professor. Halloa, Hopkins! This is very important. The professor's corridor is also lined with coconut matting.'

We passed down the passage. At the end was a short flight of steps ending in a door. Our guide knocked, and then ushered us into the professor's bedroom.

It was a very large chamber, with innumerable books, which had overflowed from the shelves and lay in piles in the corners, or were stacked all round at the base of the cases. The professor was sitting on the bed. He was a remarkable-looking person with a gaunt, aquiline face and piercing dark eyes. His hair and beard were white. The latter was curiously stained with yellow around his mouth. A cigarette glowed amid the tangle of white hair. As he held out his hand to Holmes, I noticed that it was also stained with yellow nicotine.

'A smoker, Mr Holmes?' he said, speaking in well-chosen English, with a curious little mincing accent. 'I have these cigarettes especially prepared by Ionides, of Alexandria. He sends me a thousand at a time, and I have to arrange for a fresh supply every fortnight. Bad, sir, very bad, but an old man has few pleasures. Tobacco and my work — that is all that is left to me.'

Holmes had lit a cigarette and was shooting little darting glances all over the room.

'Tobacco and my work, but now only tobacco!' the old man exclaimed. 'Who could have foreseen such a terrible catastrophe? Smith was an admirable assistant. What do you think of the matter, Mr Holmes?'

'I have not yet made up my mind.'

'I shall be indebted to you if you can throw a light where all is so dark to us.'

Holmes was pacing up and down one side of the room while the old professor was talking. I observed that he was smoking with extraordinary rapidity.

'That is my magnum opus — the pile of papers on the side table. With my weak health I do not know whether I shall ever be able to complete it, now that my assistant has been taken from me. Dear me! Mr Holmes, why, you are even a quicker smoker than me.'

Holmes smiled.

'I am a connoisseur,' he said, taking his fourth cigarette from the box. 'I will not trouble you with any lengthy cross-examination, Professor Coram, since you were in bed at the time of the crime, and could know nothing about it. I would only ask this: What do you think Smith meant by his last words: "The professor — it was she"?'

The professor shook his head.

'Susan is a simpleton. I guess Smith murmured something and she twisted his words into this meaningless message.'

'I see. You have no explanation of the tragedy?'

'Possibly an accident, possibly a suicide. It is more probable than murder.'

'But the eyeglasses?'

'A fan, a glove, glasses — who knows what article may be carried as a token or treasure when a man puts an end to his life? This gentleman speaks of footprints in the grass, but it is easy to be mistaken on such a point. As to the knife, it might well be thrown far from the unfortunate man as he fell. To me it seems that Willoughby Smith has met his fate by his own hand.'

Holmes continued to walk up and down for some time, lost in thought.

'Tell me, Professor Coram,' he said, at last, 'what is in that cupboard in the bureau?'

'Nothing that would help a thief. Family papers, letters from my poor wife, diplomas of universities. Here is the key. You can look for yourself.'

Holmes picked up the key, and looked at it for an instant, then he handed it back.

'No, I don't think that it would help me,' he said. 'I think I will go down to your garden, and work out the whole matter in my head. We won't disturb you until after lunch. At two o' clock we will come again.'

We walked up and down the garden path for some time in silence.

'Do you have a clue?' I asked, at last.

'It depends upon those cigarettes that I smoked,' he said. 'I may be mistaken. The cigarettes will show me.'

'My dear Holmes,' I exclaimed, 'how on earth —'

'Well, you may see for yourself. Ah, here is Mrs Marker! Let's enjoy five minutes of conversation with her.'

Within no time, Holmes was chatting with her as if he had known her for years.

'Yes, Mr Holmes, he does smoke something terrible. All day and sometimes all night, sir.'

'Ah!' said Holmes, 'but it kills the appetite.'

'Well, I don't know about that, sir.'

'I suppose the professor eats hardly anything?'

'Well, he is variable.'

'I bet he didn't have breakfast this morning, and won't have lunch after all those cigarettes.'

'Well, he actually ate quite a big breakfast this morning and he's ordered a good dish of cutlets for his lunch. I'm surprised myself, for since I saw Mr Smith lying there on the floor, I couldn't bear to look at food. The professor, however, hasn't let it take his appetite away.'

We spent the morning in the garden. Stanley Hopkins had gone down to the village to look into some rumours of a strange woman who had been seen by some children on the Chatham Road the previous morning. Holmes's usual energy seemed gone. Even the news brought back by Hopkins that he had found the children, and that they had undoubtedly seen a woman exactly corresponding with Holmes's description, and wearing either spectacles or eyeglasses, failed to rouse any interest. He was more attentive when Susan informed him that Mr Smith had been out

for a walk yesterday morning, and that he had only returned half an hour before the tragedy occurred. I could not see the bearing of this incident, but Holmes was weaving it into the general scheme which he had formed in his brain.

Suddenly he sprang from his chair. 'Two o'clock, gentlemen,' he said. 'We must go up and meet the professor.'

The old man had just finished his lunch, and his empty dish bore evidence to his good appetite.

'Well, Mr Holmes, have you solved this mystery yet?'

He shoved the large tin of cigarettes which stood on a table beside him towards my companion. Holmes stretched out his hand at the same moment, and the box tipped over the edge. For a few minutes we were all on our knees retrieving stray cigarettes. When we rose again, I observed Holmes's eyes were shining and his cheeks tinged with colour.

'Yes,' he said, 'I have solved it.'

Stanley Hopkins and I stared in amazement. The old professor almost sneered.

'In the garden?'

'No, here.'

'Here! When?'

'This instant.'

'You are surely joking, Mr Holmes.'

'I don't yet know what your motives are, or what exact part you play in this strange business. I'll probably hear it from you in a few minutes. Meanwhile I will reconstruct what is past for your benefit.'

'A lady yesterday entered your study. She came to take certain documents that were in your bureau. She had a key of her own. I have examined your key and it doesn't have that slight discolouration which the scratch made upon the varnish would have produced. She came without your knowledge to rob you.'

The professor blew a cloud from his lips.

'Surely you can also say what has become of her.'

'I will try to do so. In the first place she was seized by your secretary, and stabbed him in order to escape. This was most likely an unhappy accident. An assassin does not come unarmed. Horrified, she rushed away from the scene. She had, however, lost her glasses in the scuffle. She was extremely short-sighted and really helpless without them. She ran down a corridor, which she thought was same as she had come by — both were lined with coconut matting. She realized only too late that she had taken the wrong passage. She could not go back. She could not stay there. She went on and found herself in your room.'

The old man sat with his mouth open, staring wildly at Holmes. Amazement and fear were stamped upon his face. Now, with an effort, he shrugged his shoulders and burst into insincere laughter.

'There is one little flaw in your splendid theory, Mr Holmes. I was in my room all day. You mean to say that I could lie upon that bed and not be aware that a woman had entered my room?'

'I never said so. You were aware of it. You spoke with her. You recognized her. You helped her escape.'

Again the professor burst into high-keyed laughter.

'You are mad!' he cried. 'I helped her to escape? Where is she now?'

'She is there,' said Holmes, pointing to a high bookcase in the corner of the room.

The old man threw up his arms, a terrible convulsion passed over his grim face, and he fell back in his chair. At the same instant the bookcase

swung round, and a woman rushed out into the room.

'You are right!' she cried, in a strange foreign voice. 'I am here.'

She had the exact physical characteristics which Holmes had guessed. There was a certain nobility in the woman's bearing, which compelled something of respect and admiration.

Stanley Hopkins had laid his hand upon her arm and claimed her as his prisoner, but she waved him aside gently, and yet with an over-mastering dignity which compelled obedience. The old man lay back in his chair with a twitching face, and stared at her with brooding eyes.

'Yes, sir, I am your prisoner,' she said. 'I could hear everything, and I know that you have learned the truth. I confess it all. I accidentally killed the young man.'

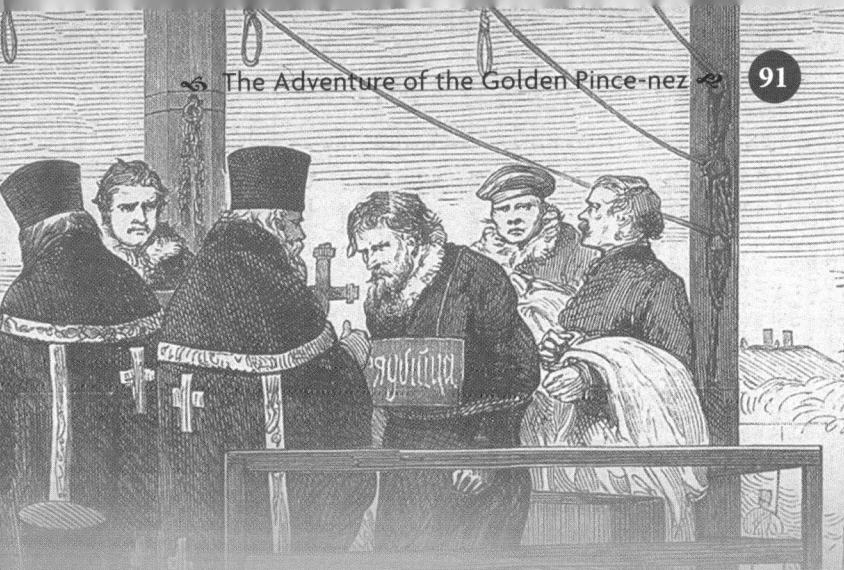

'Madam,' said Holmes, 'I don't think you are well.'

She had turned a dreadful colour. She sat down on the side of the bed and resumed.

'I want you to know the whole truth. I am this man's wife. He is not an Englishman. He is a Russian. His name I will not tell.'

'God bless you, Anna!' the old man cried.

She looked at him with the deepest disdain.

'He was fifty and I a foolish girl of twenty when we married. We were reformers — revolutionists — Nihilists, you understand. Then there came a time of trouble, a police officer was killed, many were arrested, evidence was wanted, and in order to save his own life and to earn a great reward, my husband betrayed his own wife and his companions. We were all arrested upon his

confession. Some of us were sent to the gallows, and some to Siberia. I was among these last, but my term was not for life. My husband came to England with his ill-gotten gains and has lived quietly ever since, knowing well that if the Brotherhood knew where he was justice would be done within a week.'

The old man reached out a trembling hand and helped himself to a cigarette.

'I am in your hands, Anna,' he said. 'You were always good to me.'

'I have not yet told you the height of his villainy,' she said. 'Among our comrades was a dear friend of mine. He was noble, unselfish, loving. He hated violence. He wrote forever dissuading us from such a course. These letters would have saved him. So would my diary, in which, I had entered both my feelings towards him and the view which each of us had taken. My husband found and kept both diary and letters. He hid them, and he tried hard to swear away the young man's life. He failed, but Alexis was sent a convict to Siberia, where he now works in a salt mine. Think of that, you villain! At this very moment, Alexis, a man whose name you are not worthy to speak, works and lives like a slave, and yet I have your life in my hands, and I let you go.'

'You were always a noble woman, Anna,' said the old man.

She rose, but fell back again with a little cry of pain.

'I must finish,' she said. 'When my term was over I set myself to get the diary and letters which, if sent to the Russian government, would procure my friend's release. I knew that my husband had come to England. After months of searching I discovered where he was. I engaged an agent from a private detective firm, who entered my husband's house as a secretary — it was your second secretary, Sergius, the one who left you so

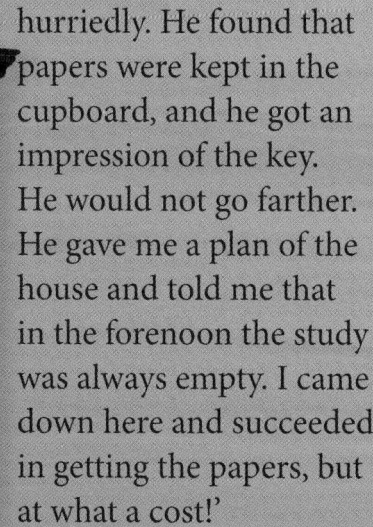

hurriedly. He found that papers were kept in the cupboard, and he got an impression of the key. He would not go farther. He gave me a plan of the house and told me that in the forenoon the study was always empty. I came down here and succeeded in getting the papers, but at what a cost!'

'I had just taken the paper; and was locking the cupboard, when the young man seized me. I had seen him already that morning. He had met me on the road, and I had asked him to tell me where Professor Coram lived, not knowing that he was his employee.'

'Exactly!' said Holmes. 'The secretary came back, and told his employer of the woman he had met. Then, in his last breath, he tried to send a message that it was she — the she whom he had just discussed with him.'

'You must let me speak,' said the woman, her face contracted as if in pain. 'When he had fallen I rushed from the room, chose the wrong door, and found myself in my husband's room. He spoke of giving me up. I showed him that his life was in my hands. If he gave me to the law, I could give him to the Brotherhood. He knew that I would do what I said. For that reason alone he shielded me. It was agreed that when the police left the house I should slip away by night and not come back. But in some way you have read our plans.' She tore from her dress a small packet.

'These are my last words,' she said, 'here is the packet which will save Alexis. I confide it to your honour and to your love of justice. Deliver it at the Russian Embassy. Now, I have done my duty, and —'

'Stop her!' cried Holmes. He bounded across the room and wrenched a small phial from her hand.

'Too late!' she said, sinking back on the bed.
'I took the poison before I left my hiding place.
I charge you, sir, to remember the packet.'

'A simple case, and yet, in some ways, an
instructive one,' Holmes remarked, as we travelled
back to town. 'It hinged from the outset upon the
pince-nez. Had the dying man not seized these, I
am not sure that we could ever have reached our
solution. It was clear to me, from the strength of
the glasses, that the wearer must have been very
blind and helpless without them. When you said
that she walked along a narrow strip of grass
without once making a false step, I remarked,
as you may remember, that it was a noteworthy
performance. In my mind I set it down as an
impossible performance, unless she had a second
pair of glasses. I was forced, therefore, to consider

seriously that she had remained within the house. On perceiving the similarity of the two corridors, it became clear that she might very easily have made such a mistake, and, in that case, she must have entered the professor's room. I examined the room narrowly for a hiding-place. The carpet seemed continuous and firmly nailed, so I dismissed the idea of a trapdoor. There might well be a secret space behind the books. Such devices are common in old libraries. I observed that books were piled on the floor at all other points, but that one bookcase was left clear. This, then, might be the door. I could see no marks to guide me, but the carpet was of a dun colour, which lends itself very well to examination. I therefore smoked a lot of cigarettes and dropped the ash all over the space in front of the suspected bookcase. I then went downstairs and confirmed that Professor Coram's consumption of food had increased — as one would expect when he is supplying a second person. We then went back to the room, when, by upsetting the cigarette box, I obtained an excellent view of the floor.It was clear from the traces upon the cigarette ash that the prisoner had come out in our absence. Well, Hopkins, I congratulate you on having brought your case to a successful conclusion. I think, Watson, you and I will drive together to the Russian Embassy.'

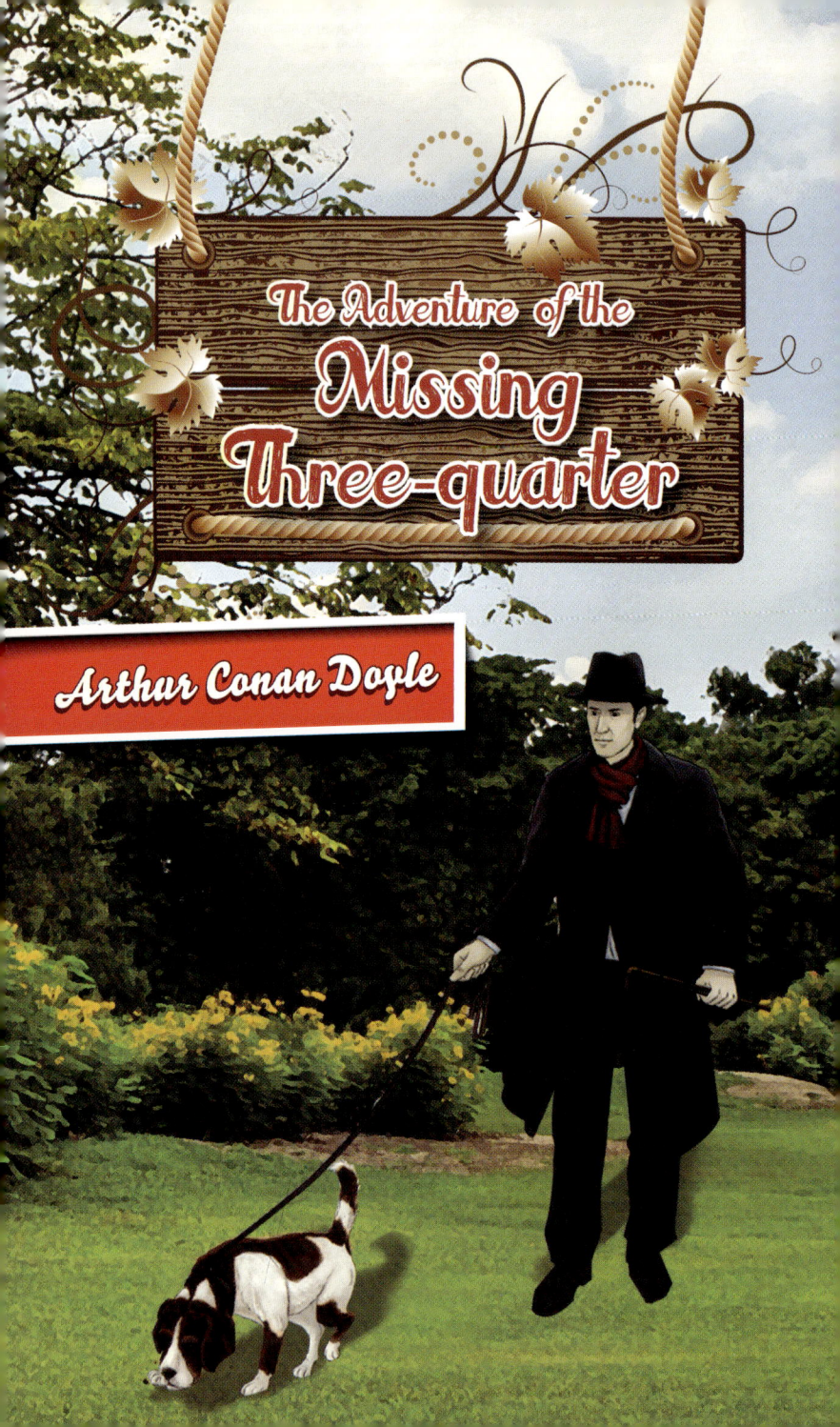

Astrange telegram reached us at Baker Street on a gloomy February morning. It was addressed to Sherlock Holmes and said:

Please await me. Terrible misfortune. Right wing three-quarter missing, indispensable tomorrow. OVERTON.

Soon thereafter the card of Mr Cyril Overton, Trinity College, Cambridge, announced the arrival of an enormous young man.

'I've been down to Scotland Yard, Mr Holmes. Inspector Stanley Hopkins advised me to come to you.'

'Pray sit down and tell me what is the matter.'

'It's awful, Mr Holmes! Godfrey Staunton – you've heard of him, of course? He's simply the hinge that the whole team turns on. We are done unless you can help me find him.'

Holmes remarked, 'Godfrey Staunton is a new name to me.'

'Great Scott!' cried Overton. 'I didn't think there was a soul in England who didn't know Godfrey Staunton, the crack three-quarter, Cambridge, Blackheath and five Internationals. Good Lord! Mr Holmes, where have you lived?'

Holmes laughed at the young giant's naive astonishment.

'You live in a different world to me, Mr Overton — a sweeter and healthier one. I beg you to sit down and to tell me exactly what has occurred.'

Young Overton laid his strange story before us.

'I am the skipper of the Rugger team of Cambridge 'Varsity, and Godfrey Staunton is my best man. Tomorrow we play Oxford. Yesterday we all came up and settled at Bentley's private hotel. At ten o'clock I went round and saw that all the fellows had gone to roost. I had a word or two with Godfrey before he turned in. He seemed to be pale and bothered. I asked him what was the matter. He said he was all right – just a touch of headache. I bade him good-night and left him. Half an hour later, the porter tells me that a rough-looking man called with a note for

Godfrey. The note was taken to his room. Godfrey read it, and fell back in a chair. The porter was so scared that he was going to fetch me, but Godfrey stopped him, had a drink of water, and pulled himself together. Then he went downstairs, said a few words to the man who was waiting in the hall, and the two of them went off together. The last that the porter saw of them, they were almost running down the street in the direction of the Strand. This morning Godfrey's room was empty and his bed had never been slept in. He had gone off at a moment's notice with this stranger, and no word has come from him since. He was a true sportsman and he wouldn't have stopped his training and let in his skipper if it were not for some cause that was too strong for him.'

Holmes listened with the deepest attention.

'What did you do?' he asked.

'I wired to Cambridge to learn if anything had been heard of him there. I have had an answer. No one has seen him. Then I wired to Lord Mount-James. Godfrey is an orphan, and Lord Mount-James is his nearest relative — his uncle, I believe.'

'This throws new light upon the matter. Lord Mount-James is one of the richest men in England.'

'Godfrey was his heir, and the old boy is nearly eighty. He never allowed Godfrey a shilling in his life, for he is an absolute miser.'

'Have you heard from Lord Mount-James?'

'No.'

'Well, I shall be happy to look into the matter,' said Holmes. 'Let us go to the hotel and talk to the porter.'

***

'You are the day porter?' asked Holmes

'Yes, sir.'

'The night porter saw nothing?'

'No, sir.'

'Were you on duty all day yesterday?'

'Yes, sir.'

'Did you take any messages to Mr Staunton?'

'Yes, sir, one telegram.'

'What o'clock was this?'

'About six.'

'Where was Mr Staunton when he received it?'

'Here in his room.'

'Were you present when he opened it?'

'Yes, sir, I waited to see if there was an answer.'

'Was there?'

'Yes, sir, he wrote an answer.'

'Did you take it?'

'No, he took it himself.'

'But he wrote it in your presence.'

'Yes, sir.'

'What did he write it with?'

'A pen, sir.'

'Was the telegraphic form one of these on the table?'

'Yes, sir, it was the top one.'

Holmes carried the forms over to the window and carefully examined the uppermost form.

'It is a pity he did not write in pencil,' said he. 'The impression usually goes through. However, I can find no trace here. But since he wrote with a broad-pointed quill pen, we will find some impression upon this blotting pad.'

He tore off a strip of the blotting paper and turned towards us the following hieroglyphic:

'The paper is thin, and the reverse will give the message. Here it is.' Holmes turned it over, and we read:

'So that is the tail end of the telegram which Godfrey Staunton dispatched within a few hours of his disappearance. There are at least six words of the message which have escaped us, but what remains — "Stand by us for God's sake!" — proves that this young man saw a formidable danger which approached him, and from which someone else could protect him. "US", mark you! Another person was involved. What is the third source from which they sought help? Our inquiry has already narrowed down to that.'

'We have only to find to whom that telegram is addressed,' I suggested.

'We might be able to do that. Meanwhile, I'd like to go through these papers which have been left upon the table.'

There were a number of letters, bills and notebooks, which Holmes turned over and examined.

'Nothing here,' he said, at last. 'By the way, I suppose your friend was a healthy young fellow?'

'Sound as a bell.'

'Have you ever known him ill?'

'Not a day.'

'Perhaps he was not that strong. He may have had some secret trouble. With your assent, I will put one or two of these papers in my pocket.'

'One moment!' cried a bitter voice, and we looked up to find a queer little old man in the doorway. He was dressed in rusty black, with a very broad-brimmed top hat and a loose white necktie. In spite of his shabby appearance, his voice had a sharp crackle, and his manner a quick intensity which commanded attention.

'Who are you, sir, and by what right do you touch this gentleman's papers?' he asked.

'I am a private detective, and I am trying to explain his disappearance.'

'And who instructed you?'

'This gentleman, Mr Staunton's friend, was referred to me by Scotland Yard.'

'Who are you, sir?'

'I am Cyril Overton.'

'Then it is you who sent me a telegram. My name is Lord Mount-James. I came round as quickly as the Bayswater bus would bring me. So you have instructed a detective?'

'Yes, sir.'

'And are you prepared to meet the cost?'

'I have no doubt, sir, that my friend Godfrey, when we find him, will be prepared to do that.'

'But if he is never found?'

'In that case, no doubt his family —'

'Nothing of the sort, sir!' screamed the little man. 'Don't look to me for a penny! You understand that, Mr Detective! I have never wasted money, and I do not propose to begin to do so now.'

'Very good, sir,' said Sherlock Holmes. 'Do you have any theory to account for this young man's disappearance?'

'No, sir. He is big enough and old enough to look after himself, and if he is so foolish as to lose himself, I entirely refuse to accept the responsibility of hunting for him.'

'I quite understand,' said Holmes, with a mischievous twinkle in his eyes. 'It is, however, entirely possible that a gang of thieves have secured your nephew in order to gain from him some information as to your house, your habits, and your treasure.'

The face of our unpleasant little visitor turned as white as his neck tie.

'I never thought of that! I'll have the plate moved over to the bank this evening. In the meantime spare no pains, Mr Detective! I beg you to leave no stone unturned to bring him safely back. As to money, well, so far as a fiver or even a tenner goes you can always look to me.'

The noble miser, however, could not give us any helpful information, for he knew little of the private life of his nephew. Our only clue lay in the truncated telegram.

There was a telegraph office at a short distance from the hotel. We halted outside it.

'It's worth trying, Watson,' said Holmes. 'I don't suppose they remember faces in such a busy place.'

'I am sorry to trouble you,' said he to the young woman behind the grating, 'there is some small mistake about a telegram I sent yesterday. I have had no answer, and I very much fear that I must have omitted to put my name at the end. Could you tell me if this was so?'

The young woman turned over a sheaf of counterfoils.

'What o'clock was it?' she asked.

'A little after six.'

'Whom was it to?'

Holmes put his finger to his lips and glanced at me.

'The last words in it were "For God's sake,"' he whispered, confidentially, 'I am very anxious at getting no answer.'

The young woman separated one of the forms.

'This is it. There is no name,' said she, smoothing it out upon the counter.

'Then that, of course, accounts for my getting no answer,' said Holmes. 'How very stupid of me!'

He chuckled and rubbed his hands when we found ourselves in the street once more.

'Well?' I asked.

'We have gained a starting point for our investigation. We must run down to Cambridge together.'

It was already dark when we reached the old university city. Holmes took a cab at the station and ordered the man to drive to the house of Dr Leslie Armstrong. A few minutes later, we had stopped at a large mansion. After a long wait we were admitted into the consulting room, where we found the doctor seated behind his table.

Even without knowing his brilliant record one could not fail to be impressed by a mere glance at the man. He did not look very pleased.

'I have come to ask you about Mr Godfrey Staunton,' said Holmes.

'What about him?'

'You know him?'

'He is an intimate friend of mine.'

'You are aware that he has disappeared?'

'Ah, indeed!'

There was no change of expression in the rugged features of the doctor.

'He left his hotel last night — he has not been heard of.'

'No doubt he will return.'

'Tomorrow is the 'varsity football match.'

'I have no sympathy with these childish games.'

'I claim your sympathy, then, in my investigation of Mr Staunton's fate. Do you know where he is?'

'Certainly not.'

'You have not seen him since yesterday?'

'No, I have not.'

'Was Mr Staunton a healthy man?'

'Absolutely.'

'Did you ever know him ill?'

'Never.'

Holmes popped a sheet of paper before the doctor's eyes. 'Then perhaps you will explain this receipted bill for thirteen guineas, paid by Mr Godfrey Staunton last month to Dr Leslie Armstrong, of Cambridge. I picked it out from among the papers upon his desk.'

The doctor flushed with anger.

'I do not feel that there is any reason why I should offer an explanation to you, Mr Holmes.'

Holmes replaced the bill in his notebook. 'You would really be wiser to take me into your complete confidence.'

'I know nothing about it.'

'Did you hear from Mr Staunton in London?'

'Certainly not.'

'An urgent telegram was dispatched to you from London by Godfrey Staunton at 6:15 yesterday evening — a telegram which is undoubtedly associated with his disappearance—and yet you have not had it. I shall certainly go down to the post office here and register a complaint.'

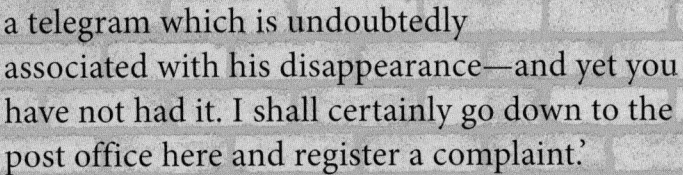

Dr Leslie Armstrong sprang up from behind his desk, and his dark face was crimson with fury.

'Walk out of my house, sir,' said he.

'You can tell your employer, Lord Mount-James, that I do not wish to have anything to do either with him or with his agents.'

He rang the bell furiously.

'John, show these gentlemen out!'

A pompous butler ushered us severely to the door, and we found ourselves in the street. Holmes burst out laughing.

'Dr Leslie Armstrong is certainly a man of energy and character,' said he. 'This little inn just opposite Armstrong's house is singularly adapted to our needs. If you would engage a front room and purchase the necessaries for the night, I may have time to make a few inquiries.'

Holmes did not return to the inn until nearly nine o'clock. He was pale and dejected, stained with dust, and exhausted with hunger and fatigue. A cold supper was ready upon the table. The sound of carriage wheels caused him to rise and glance out of the window. A carriage and pair of grays, under the glare of a gas lamp, stood before the doctor's door.

'It's been out three hours,' said Holmes, 'started at half-past six, and here it is back again. That gives a radius of ten or twelve miles, and he does it once, or sometimes twice, a day.'

'No unusual thing for a doctor in practice.'

'But Armstrong is not really a doctor in practice. He is a lecturer and a consultant, but he does not care for general practice, which distracts him from his literary work. Why, then, does he make these long journeys, which must be exceedingly irksome to him, and who is it that he visits?'

'His coachman —'

'My dear Watson, can you doubt that it was to him that I first applied? He was rude enough to set a dog at me. Neither dog nor man liked the look of my stick, however, and the matter fell through. Relations were strained after that, and further enquiries are out of the question. All that I have learned I got from a friendly native in the yard of our own inn. It was he who told me of the doctor's daily journey. At that instant the carriage came round to the door.'

'Couldn't you follow it?'

'The idea did cross my mind. I rushed into the bicycle shop next to our inn and engaged a bicycle. I rapidly overtook the carriage, and then, keeping at a discreet distance of a hundred yards or so, I followed its lights until we were clear of the town. We had got well out on the country road, when the carriage stopped. The doctor alighted, walked swiftly back to where I had also halted, and told me that he feared the road was narrow, and that he hoped his carriage did not impede the passage of my bicycle. Nothing could have been more admirable than his way of putting it. I at once rode past the carriage, and, keeping to the main road, I went on for a few miles, and then halted in a convenient place to see if the carriage passed. There was no sign of it, however, and so it became evident that it had turned down one of several side roads which I had observed. I rode back, but again saw nothing of the carriage, and now it has returned after me. I had no particular reason to connect these journeys with the disappearance of Godfrey Staunton. I was only inclined to investigate them on the general grounds that everything which concerns Dr Armstrong is of interest to us. Now that I find he keeps so keen a look-out upon anyone who may follow him on these excursions, the affair appears more important.'

'We can follow him tomorrow.'

'It is not that easy. Cambridgeshire scenery does not lend itself to concealment. All this country that I passed over tonight is as flat and clean as the palm of your hand, and the man we are following is no fool, as he very clearly showed tonight. I have wired to Overton to let us know any fresh London developments at this address, and in the meantime we can only concentrate our attention upon Dr Armstrong, whose name the obliging young lady at the office allowed me to read upon the counterfoil of Staunton's urgent message. He certainly knows where the young man is.'

The next day a note was handed in after breakfast, which Holmes passed across to me with a smile.

SIR

I can assure you that you are wasting your time in dogging my movements. I have, as you discovered last night, a window at the back of my brougham, and if you desire a twenty-mile ride which will lead you to the spot from which you started, you have only to follow me. Meanwhile, I can inform you that no spying upon me can in any way help Mr Godfrey Staunton, and I am convinced that the best service you can do to that gentleman is to return at once to London and to report to your employer that you are unable to trace him. Your time in Cambridge will certainly be wasted.

Yours faithfully,

LESLIE ARMSTRONG.

'An outspoken, honest antagonist,' said Holmes. 'I am going to make some independent explorations of my own.'

My friend came back at night weary and unsuccessful.

'I have had a blank day, Watson. Having got the doctor's general direction, I spent the day visiting all the villages upon that side of Cambridge, and comparing notes with publicans and other local news agencies. They have all proved disappointing. The daily appearance of a carriage and pair could hardly have been overlooked in such Sleepy Hollows. The doctor has scored once more. Is there a telegram for me?'

'Yes, I opened it. Here it is: "Ask for Pompey from Jeremy Dixon, Trinity College."'

'I don't understand it.'

'Oh, it is from our friend Overton, and is in answer to a question from me. I'll just send round a note to Mr Jeremy Dixon, and then I have no doubt that our luck will turn. By the way, is there any news of the match?'

'Yes, the local evening paper has an excellent account. Oxford won by a goal and two tries. The last sentences of the description say: "The defeat of the Light Blues may be entirely attributed to the

unfortunate absence of the crack International, Godfrey Staunton, whose want was felt at every instant of the game."'

'Then our friend Overton's forebodings have been justified,' said Holmes.

Next morning, Holmes sat by the fire holding his tiny hypodermic syringe.

'On this syringe I base all my hopes,' he said. 'I propose to get upon Dr Armstrong's trail today.'

'He is making an early start,' said I. 'His carriage is at the door.'

'Let him go. I will now introduce you to a detective who is a very eminent specialist in the work that lies before us.'

I followed Holmes into the stable yard, where he opened the door of a loose box and led out a squat, lop-eared, white-and-tan dog, something between a beagle and a fox hound.

'Let me introduce you to Pompey,' said he. 'Pompey is the pride of the local drag-hounds. Now, boy, come along, and show what you can do.'

He led him across to the doctor's door. The dog sniffed round for an instant, and then with a shrill whine of excitement started off down the street, tugging at his leash in his efforts to go faster. In half an hour, we were clear of the town and hastening down a country road.

'What have you done, Holmes?' I asked.

'I walked into the doctor's yard this morning, and shot my syringe full of aniseed over the hind wheel. A draghound will follow aniseed from here to John o'Groat's, and our friend, Armstrong, would have to drive through the Cam before he would shake Pompey off his trail. Oh, the cunning rascal! This is how he gave me the slip the other night.'

The dog had suddenly turned out of the main road into a grass-grown lane. Half a mile farther this opened into another broad road, and the trail turned hard to the right in the direction of the town, which we had just quitted. The road took a sweep to the south of the town, and continued in the opposite direction to that in which we started.

'This detour has been entirely for our benefit, then?' said Holmes. 'No wonder that my inquiries among those villagers led to nothing. This should be the village of Trumpington to the right of us. And here is the brougham coming round the corner. Quick, Watson!'

He sprang through a gate into a field, dragging the reluctant Pompey after him. We had hardly got under the shelter of the hedge when the carriage rattled past. I caught a glimpse of Dr Armstrong within, his shoulders bowed, his head sunk on his hands, the very image of distress.

'I fear there is some dark ending to our quest,' said Holmes. 'Come, Pompey! Ah, it is the cottage in the field!'

We had reached the end of our journey. Pompey ran about and whined eagerly outside the gate, where the marks of the brougham's wheels could still be seen. A footpath led across to the lonely cottage. Holmes tied the dog to the hedge,

and we hastened onward. My friend knocked at the door, without response. The cottage was not deserted, for a low sound came to our ears—a kind of drone of misery and despair. Holmes glanced back at the road. A carriage was coming down it.

'The doctor is coming back!' cried Holmes. 'We need to see what it means before he comes.'

He opened the door, and we stepped into the hall. The droning sound came from upstairs. Holmes darted up, and I followed him. He pushed open a half-closed door, and we both stood shocked at the sight before us.

A woman, young and beautiful, was lying dead upon the bed. At the foot of the bed was a young man, whose frame was racked by his sobs. So absorbed was he by his bitter grief, that he never looked up until Holmes's hand was on his shoulder.

'Are you Mr Godfrey Staunton?'

'Yes, I am but you are too late. She is dead.'

The man was so dazed that he could not be made to understand that we were anything but doctors who had been sent to his assistance. Holmes was trying to utter a few words of consolation when there was a step upon the stairs, and there was the heavy, stern, questioning face of Dr Armstrong at the door.

'So, gentlemen,' said he, 'you have attained your end and have certainly chosen a particularly delicate moment for your intrusion.'

'Excuse me, Dr Armstrong, if you could step downstairs with us, we may each be able to give some light to the other upon this miserable affair.'

A minute later, we were in the sitting-room below.

'I wish you to understand that I am not employed by Lord Mount-James. When a man is lost it is my duty to ascertain his fate, but having done so the matter ends so far as I am concerned, and so long as there is nothing criminal I am much more anxious to hush up private scandals than to give them publicity. If there is no breach of the law, you can absolutely depend upon my discretion and my cooperation in keeping the facts out of the papers.'

Dr Armstrong took a quick step forward and wrung Holmes by the hand.

'I had misjudged you,' said he. 'A year ago Godfrey Staunton stayed in London for a time and became passionately attached to his landlady's daughter, whom he married. But Godfrey was the heir to this crabbed old nobleman, and it was quite certain that the news of his marriage would have been the end of his inheritance. I knew the lad well, and I loved him for his many excellent qualities. We did our very best to keep the thing from everyone. Their secret was known to no one save to me and to one excellent servant, who has at present gone for assistance to Trumpington. But at last there came a terrible blow in the shape of dangerous illness to his wife. It was consumption of the most severe kind. The poor boy was half crazed with grief, and yet he had to go to London to play this match, for he could not get out of it without explanations which would expose his secret. I tried to cheer him up by wire, and he sent me one in reply, imploring me to do all I could. This was the telegram which you appear in some inexplicable way to have seen. I did not tell him how urgent the danger was, for I knew that he could do no good here, but I sent the truth to the girl's father, and he very injudiciously communicated it to Godfrey. The result was that he came straight away in a state bordering on frenzy, and has remained in the same state, kneeling at the end of her bed, until this morning death put an end to her sufferings. I am sure, Mr Holmes, that I can rely upon your discretion and that of your friend.'

Holmes grasped the doctor's hand.

'Come, Watson,' said he, and we passed from that house of grief into the pale sunlight of the winter day.

Other Titles *In the* Series

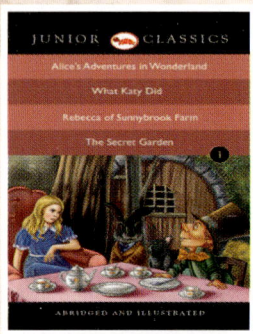

JUNIOR CLASSICS

Alice's Adventures in Wonderland

What Katy Did

Rebecca of Sunnybrook Farm

The Secret Garden

1

ABRIDGED AND ILLUSTRATED

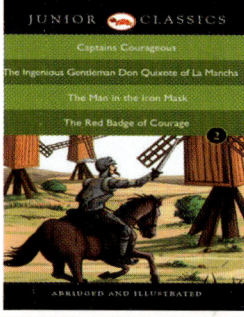

JUNIOR CLASSICS

Captains Courageous

The Ingenious Gentleman Don Quixote of La Mancha

The Man in the Iron Mask

The Red Badge of Courage

2

ABRIDGED AND ILLUSTRATED

JUNIOR CLASSICS

The Call of the Wild

Moby Dick or the Whale

The Little Mermaid

Animal Farm

3

ABRIDGED AND ILLUSTRATED

JUNIOR CLASSICS

Heidi

A Tale of Two Cities

Little Women

Black Beauty

4

ABRIDGED AND ILLUSTRATED

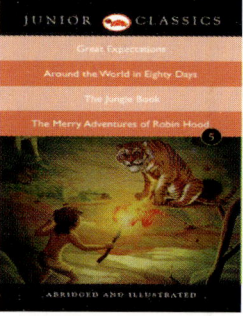

JUNIOR CLASSICS

Great Expectations

Around the World in Eighty Days

The Jungle Book

The Merry Adventures of Robin Hood

5

ABRIDGED AND ILLUSTRATED

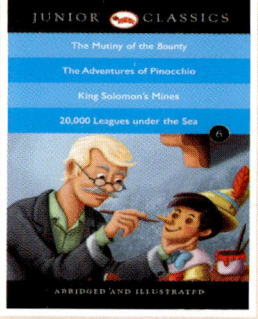

JUNIOR CLASSICS

The Mutiny of the Bounty

The Adventures of Pinocchio

King Solomon's Mines

20,000 Leagues under the Sea

6

ABRIDGED AND ILLUSTRATED

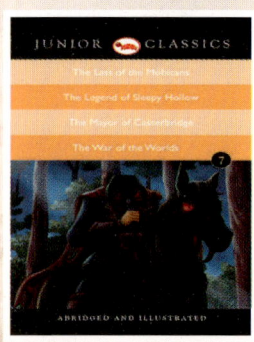

JUNIOR CLASSICS

The Last of the Mohicans

The Legend of Sleepy Hollow

The Mayor of Casterbridge

The War of the Worlds

7

ABRIDGED AND ILLUSTRATED

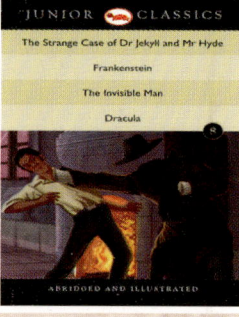

JUNIOR CLASSICS

The Strange Case of Dr Jekyll and Mr Hyde

Frankenstein

The Invisible Man

Dracula

8

ABRIDGED AND ILLUSTRATED

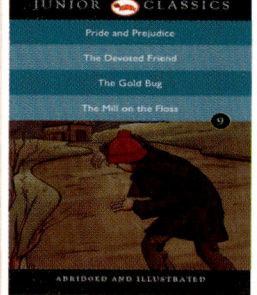

JUNIOR CLASSICS

Pride and Prejudice

The Devoted Friend

The Gold Bug

The Mill on the Floss

9

ABRIDGED AND ILLUSTRATED